Dragonflies

Written by Jo Windsor

A dragonfly is a big insect.
It has four big wings.
Look at the dragonfly's wings.

4 wings

wings

A dragonfly is good at flying.
It will fly very fast to get away
from birds.

(It can fly up to 60mph.)

bird

dragonfly

5

A dragonfly has big eyes.
It can see very well with its eyes.
It can see better than
all other insects.

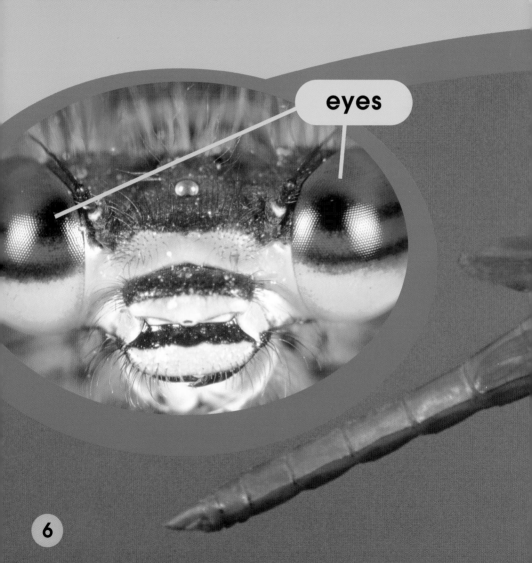

eyes

A dragonfly can see things
that are still.
It can see things
that are moving, too.

eye

A dragonfly hunts for its food.
It flies in the air and swoops
down to catch its food.

A dragonfly catches its food
with its legs.
It holds the food in its legs
like a basket.

A dragonfly lays its eggs
in the water.
The eggs hatch into
little dragonflies.

The little dragonflies
live under the water.
They do not have wings.

Little dragonflies
are called nymphs.

water

A little dragonfly eats fish and tadpoles for its food.

The little dragonfly will grow. It will grow bigger and bigger. It has to come out of its skin.

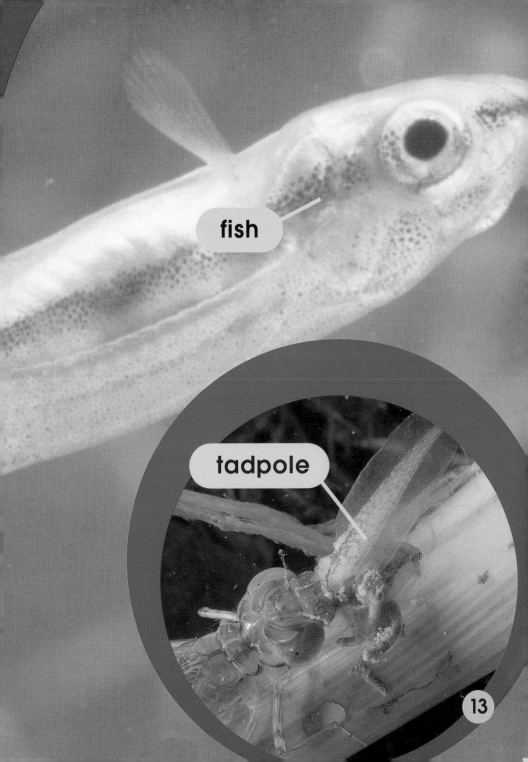

fish

tadpole

13

Look at the little dragonfly now.
It comes out of the water.
It comes out of its skin.

Now the dragonfly has wings.
It can fly away.

Index

Guide Notes

Title: Dragonflies
Stage: Early (4) – Green

Genre: Nonfiction
Approach: Guided Reading
Processes: Thinking Critically, Exploring Language, Processing Information
Written and Visual Focus: Photographs (static images), Caption, Labels, Index
Word Count: 194

THINKING CRITICALLY
(sample questions)
- Ask the children what they think this book could be about.
- Look at the title and read it to the children. Ask the children: "What do you think this book is going to tell us?"
- Ask the children what they know about dragonflies.
- Focus the children's attention on the index. Ask: "What are you going to find out about in this book?"
- If you want to find out about wings, on which pages would you look?
- If you want to find out about eyes, on which pages would you look?
- Do you think a dragonfly could carry an apple? Why? Why not?
- How do you think a little dragonfly gets out of its skin?

EXPLORING LANGUAGE

Terminology
Title, cover, photographs, author, photographers

Vocabulary
Interest words: insect, wings, hunt, swoops, basket, skin
High-frequency words: things, catch
Compound words: dragonfly, away, into
Positional words: down, into, in, under, out

Print Conventions
Capital letter for sentence beginnings, periods, comma, parenthesis